WITHDRAWN

ORCA

J Guest
Guest, Jacqueline
Secret signs
SM
$5.95
ocm70231792
11/17/2010

SECRET SIGNS

Jacqueline Guest

☺H!

ORCA BOOK PUBLISHERS

Copyright 2006 © Jacqueline Guest

All rights reserved. No part of this publication may be reproduced or transmitted in any form or by any means, electronic or mechanical, including photocopying, recording or by any information storage and retrieval system now known or to be invented, without permission in writing from the publisher.

Library and Archives Canada Cataloguing in Publication

Guest, Jacqueline

Secret signs / Jacqueline Guest.

(Orca young readers)
ISBN 1-55143-599-3

I. Title.

PS8563.U365S42 2006 jC813'.54 C2006-903446-X

First published in the United States, 2006

Library of Congress Control Number: 2006928964

Summary: During the Depression, Henry Dafoe makes his way across the prairies, guided only by an old hobo and a series of secret signs.

Free teachers' guide available: www.orcabook.com

Orca Book Publishers gratefully acknowledges the support for its publishing programs provided by the following agencies: the Government of Canada through the Book Publishing Industry Development Program and the Canada Council for the Arts, and the Province of British Columbia through the BC Arts Council and the Book Publishing Tax Credit.

Cover design by Doug McCaffry
Cover & interior illustrations by June Lawrason
Secret signs by S. N. Harvey

In Canada:
Orca Book Publishers
Box 5626 Stn. B
Victoria, BC Canada
V8R 6S4

In the United States:
Orca Book Publishers
PO Box 468
Custer, WA USA
98240-0468

www.orcabook.com
Printed and bound in Canada.
Printed on recycled paper.
09 08 07 06 • 6 5 4 3 2 1

For Tyler

Joy, laughter and magic, all in one tiny person.

Here's a book full of trains just for you.

The author would like to thank the Alberta Foundation for the Arts for its support in the writing of this book.

Contents

Chapter 1	A Kindhearted Woman Lives Here 1
Chapter 2	Hit the Road Quick! 10
Chapter 3	There Are Thieves About 22
Chapter 4	Well-guarded Home 30
Chapter 5	A Cranky Man Lives Here 35
Chapter 6	An Officer of the Law Lives Here 46
Chapter 7	Be Quiet! 56
Chapter 8	Road Spoiled 65
Chapter 9	Generous People 76
Chapter 10	Doctor Won't Charge for His Services 84
Chapter 11	Man With a Gun Lives Here 95
Chapter 12	Here You Will Find Friends 104
Chapter 13	A Good Place for Sit-down Food 113
Chapter 14	Don't Give Up 122
Chapter 15	A Good Road to Follow 129
	Key to the secret signs 140

CHAPTER 1

The air grew strangely still, and the hair on the back of Henry Dafoe's neck stood straight up. He sucked in his breath. Marching toward him across the parched prairie was a towering black wall that blotted out the sun.

He and his little sister, Anne, were walking home after school on the path that skirted a shallow lake, now nearly dry. The baked mud at the edge of the water was cracked and lined like the face of an old man.

"Come on, Anne, we've got to run!" Henry yelled as he grabbed her wrist.

"Stop it, Henry! You'll crinkle the picture I made for Mama." Anne jerked her arm out of her brother's grasp.

Henry hated babysitting his sister, especially when she wouldn't listen, which was nearly all the time. He pointed at the dark curtain that stretched across the horizon. "If you don't get a move on, you'll be swallowed up by that dust cloud, and then what will happen to your precious picture?"

Anne's blue eyes grew wide with fear. She scanned the shore, then darted away, running toward an old boat stuck in the mud at the lake's edge. "Henry, let's take the rowboat! It's only ten minutes across the lake."

"We're not taking any stupid boat. We have to make a run for it!" He tried again to grasp his sister's arm, but she was too fast for him.

"It will take us a million years to get home along the path," she argued, tears welling in her eyes. "The boat is right here! Why can't we take it? Henry, I'm scared!"

"Don't be such a big baby," Henry growled. "You think you can turn on the waterworks and get whatever you want? Well, think again. Now, come on!"

He lunged for her arm, missed again and accidentally knocked his sister backward into the shallow slough. Her dress immediately became the same dirty gray as the stagnant water that swirled around her. The picture of the bright red flowers sank to the silty bottom and dissolved in a slurry of wet paint and mud.

"Serves you right for not listening." Henry glared at his soggy sister. The breeze had picked up, and he glanced at the darkening sky. "Stay if you want, but I'm leaving." He turned to go.

Henry wanted to run, but he knew his mother would be angry if he abandoned his sister, so he waited while Anne struggled out of the water, her wails carried away on the howling storm. Gripping his sister's muddy hand, he dragged her to the safety of their farm.

The wind was a black fist hammering their house. Henry doodled in his journal and tried to ignore the moaning gale. Even though the windows and doors were closed tight, fine dust drifted in and settled on the picture he'd drawn.

The drawing was of something his pa called a hobo sign—a symbol usually written in chalk or coal on a fencepost or gate. The signs directed tramps to a meal or a place to sleep or warned them of trouble in the area. His father said that a lot of hobos couldn't read, so the signs were a good way of communicating.

No one had ever told Henry what the signs meant, but he was sure he'd figured out some of their meanings. He prided himself on being extremely clever and wasn't shy about letting folks know just how smart he was, but his quick tongue often got him into a lot of trouble. Grown-ups were always telling him he was too smart for his own good. Henry studied the hobo sign he was working on. He'd seen it scribbled on the fence near Mr. Fitzwilliam's house.

It looked like a gentleman's top hat, and since Mr. Fitzwilliam was an undertaker and wore a tall black hat, Henry assumed the symbol meant that you were in the right place if you were planning a funeral.

"Henry, put that away, dear," his mother admonished as she dished up the soup they were having for supper.

"Yes, ma'am." Henry slid the journal under his behind. He looked into his bowl and sniffed, then wrinkled his nose in distaste. Cabbage soup again! He knew money was tight and they had a lot of cabbage down in the root cellar. *Waste not, want not* was his mother's motto, and they sure weren't going to waste any money...or cabbages either.

"Is there any bread?" he asked. Henry knew that unless Mama had baked more, the only two pieces in the house were the ones he'd hidden yesterday in the bottom of the empty pie safe.

His mother shook her head, then smiled at him. "I'll bake more tomorrow. Now eat your soup."

Henry felt bad about hiding the bread, but he needed the extra food. He was the man of the house now that his father had gone to Winnipeg to find work. He was the one who had to do the chores around the farm, especially since his mother had gotten sick.

Of course, chores weren't like they used to be. It was 1932, and he was only twelve, but even he remembered a time when the crops weren't being burnt up every year in the never-ending drought. Back then, he and Pa had worked together to bring in the harvest. He'd helped run the big belt-driven threshing machine, but since they hadn't planted this year, there wouldn't be any crop to harvest. His father had said the whole country was in something called the Depression. Henry didn't know exactly what the Depression had to do with them, but he did know that they didn't have nearly as many nice things as they used to.

"Mama, guess who I saw today?" Henry ignored the wind clawing at the windows.

"The Thompsons—and you should see what they've done to our car."

"That car isn't ours anymore," his mother reminded him.

Their shiny black car had been sold to the neighbors, but the Thompsons had fallen on tough times. "They've cut the roof off," he continued, "and rigged that car up so their team of horses can pull it down the road without the engine running. Can you believe it?"

His mother looked thoughtful. "I heard they'd turned it into a Bennett Buggy. That's too bad, but gasoline is expensive. You have to feed horses whether you use them or not. They may as well earn their keep."

With the car gone and only their unreliable pickup left to drive, they were stuck on the farm, another thing Henry hated. Mama said they had no money for frivolous things like candy or store-bought clothes, so going into town was pointless.

"It seems strange to name that crazy contraption after the prime minister."

Henry gave his sister a superior smile as he pushed his thick brown hair out of his eyes. He enjoyed showing off his abundant knowledge.

"I know the prime minister's name, so there, Mr. Know-it-all Henry Dafoe." Anne stuck her tongue out at him. There was a stringy piece of cabbage stuck to it.

"That's a surprise, since you're such a baby!" Henry sneered.

"Am not," said Anne, her lower lip trembling.

"Stop your bickering, both of you! Anne, finish your soup." His mother pushed her bowl away and sighed wearily. "Henry, I expect better of you. Honestly, some days I'm at my wits' end with you two."

Henry glanced at his mother. She hadn't touched her soup, and her face had an alarming gray tinge that reminded him of his grandma's skin right before she died. His mama had been coughing a lot lately, and she was always tired. Henry wondered how sick she really was and when she was going to get better.

This was not how he'd imagined today would go. Henry had hoped his mother would stop treating him like a child now that Pa was gone and he was doing all the chores, but that wasn't happening. In fact, Henry thought he should get a reward for all his extra work, but that wasn't happening either. It just wasn't fair.

CHAPTER 2

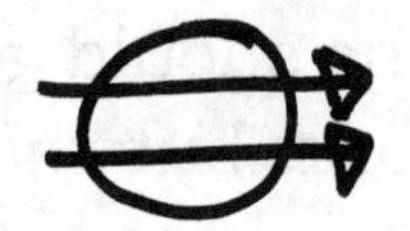

The next morning dawned bright and sunny with not a cloud in the sky. Henry pulled on his clothes and did his morning chores. When he came into the kitchen carrying the egg basket, his mother had breakfast waiting. He washed his hands and sat down at the table.

"Just in time, dear. Hot porridge—with a little brown sugar I found to sprinkle on top." His mother set a steaming bowl in front of him.

It wasn't porridge weather, but that didn't stop Henry from gobbling down first one bowl and then another.

His mother waited while they ate, then looked at him and Anne. "I have some news," she began. "Yesterday the doctor stopped by to tell me the results of those fancy tests he did."

Henry leaned his elbow on the table and listened, just as his papa would have done if he were here. After all, as the man of the house he should know just how sick his mother was.

Anne shot Henry an angry glance. "I painted a picture to make you feel better, Mama, but it got wrecked when Henry *pushed* me in the lake yesterday."

"It was your own fault," he snapped back.

"Now, children," his mother interrupted tiredly. "Anne, I'm sure Henry did what he thought best. He's the oldest and you should mind him."

Henry grinned at his sister.

His mother continued, "The doctor says I have to go into a special hospital for folks with bad lungs. The hospital's a long way from here."

"How far away, Mama?" Anne asked, her voice small and anxious.

Their mother's brow furrowed. "It takes us an hour to drive to Winnipeg, and the hospital is another two hours farther south. I'll be there for a long time—many months."

Henry and Anne stared at her.

"What's going to happen to me?" Henry burst out, then glanced guiltily at his little sister. "I mean, who's going to take care of *us*?"

His mother sighed. "I've worked it all out. Anne, I've made arrangements for you to stay with the Sisters of Mercy in Winnipeg."

Anne clapped her hands. "I loved going to the convent school last year. Mother Superior always gave the farm girls an extra slice of orange at lunch. Going to the little school at the crossroads this year hasn't been nearly as much fun." She grinned smugly at Henry and then slurped her porridge noisily.

"We'll do whatever it takes to help out, won't we, Anne?" Henry thought he sounded very grown up. With Anne gone, his life would be so much better. His mother turned to him. "I'm glad you see it that way, Henry, because tomorrow you'll leave to stay with your Uncle Paul in Nova Scotia. He says he can use a strong boy like you on his fishing boat this summer. I'll send money for your upkeep. Think of the wonderful experience you'll have being a fisherman."

Henry was shocked. His mother was smiling as though she truly believed her solution was a good one. She was going to send him away to work on a horrible, smelly, scary fishing boat! The idea of being on the water every day made his stomach lurch; the porridge rose ominously in his throat.

It had all started last spring when he'd lied to his teacher and said he had to go to his aunt's funeral. He and Jimmy Hutchins had gone to the creek, and he'd been showing off, diving in head first, forgetting the water level was very low. He'd hit his head on a rock and nearly drowned. If Jimmy hadn't dragged him to shore, he'd have been a goner for sure. Ever since that terrifying day, he couldn't even think of going swimming without feeling sick. The thought of spending every waking minute on a boat was horrifying.

Henry swallowed, his throat tight. If he hadn't been playing hooky, he could have told his parents what had happened, and they'd have given him the special treatment a near-drowning victim deserves.

One thing was certain. He could not work on his uncle's or any other boat! "I can't go to Nova Scotia, Mama. It's too far away. I'd miss you and Anne so much, why, I'd be heartsick. I might die!" His voice cracked and he looked at his mother, silently praying she'd let him stay.

Henry's mother patted his hand. "I know you don't want to leave, dear, but there's no other way. It's all arranged. Tomorrow we'll drive Anne to the convent and then I'll drop you at the bus station."

"We'll *both* do whatever it takes to help out, won't we, Henry?" Anne grinned at him and Henry kicked her under the table.

He thought of the boat and the deep cold sea. Spidery legs of terror crawled up his spine, and his blood chilled. "No! You can't send me away! I won't go! Do you hear me, Mother? *I won't go!*" He was yelling, and his mother stared at him, wide-eyed with astonishment.

"It's not open for discussion," she said, "and I'll thank you to remember your manners, young man. As long as you're in my house, you will show me the respect I deserve. Is that understood?"

Henry felt his face go red. He was so angry he could have spit. "Yes, ma'am," he answered contritely, but he was already plotting his escape.

That night Henry waited until everyone was asleep, then crept out of bed and inched down the stairs, avoiding the one that creaked. His book bag was slung over his shoulder, but he'd left his tedious schoolwork in his room. He needed the bag for more important cargo.

"What are you doing?"

Anne's voice in the darkness made Henry jump. She was sitting on the top stair watching him. "Shh, you'll wake Mama!" he whispered.

"Why are you dressed in the middle of the night?" Anne looked very small in her long nightgown, her tousled hair like a blond halo gone askew.

With a sigh, Henry went to sit beside his little sister. "Anne, Mama's real sick so we have to help her. The nuns will take good care of you, but Mama can't afford to send money to Uncle Paul. It's better if I find work near here, like Papa did, and that means I have to leave for a while. But it has to be our secret."

Anne looked at him with enormous eyes. "Where are you going?" she asked. "And when will you come back?" She sniffled, and Henry knew she was about to cry. He put his arm around her thin shoulders.

"Don't worry, I won't be gone forever. Tell you what. When I'm away I'll write and tell you all about my adventures. Would that make you feel better?"

Anne looked up at him and beamed. "Honest? Real letters!" Her smile faded. "But I can't read very well."

As tears welled again in his sister's eyes, Henry remembered the hobos' secret signs. Reaching into his book bag, he took out his journal. "Here," he said as he tore a page out of the book. "These are hobo signs. I'll use them to tell you about my adventures. I just need to make a set for myself." After Henry had copied all the signs into his journal, he explained their meanings to Anne. He pointed to one that looked like a cat. "If I draw a picture of a kitty, you'll know I ran into a pack of ferocious wildcats and I had to fight my way out."

Anne held the page reverently. "It will be our secret code! This will be so much fun." Then her face grew solemn again. "But what about Mama? She'll be so worried."

Henry felt a quick stab of guilt. He began writing on a fresh sheet of paper. "Give this to Mama tomorrow after breakfast—

not a minute sooner. It explains where I've gone so she won't worry." He ripped the note out of the journal and handed it to his sister. "Now, back to bed with you."

Anne hugged her brother goodbye. "I can hardly wait for my first letter," she whispered before she scampered down the hall to her room. Henry sighed with relief when she closed her door. That had been close. He put his journal back in the bag and continued downstairs.

Quietly, he gathered the things he'd need. He collected the bread slices from the pie safe, added cheese and meat, then wrapped everything in a piece of waxed paper. He stuffed the food into the bag with his journal, a change of clothes and his favorite story, *The Adventures of Tom Sawyer* by Mr. Mark Twain.

Next he went to the shelf in the living room and retrieved the special book he wasn't supposed to touch. Inside was a hollowed-out compartment where his mother kept money. Henry took ten one-dollar bills from the small stack, hesitated and put five back. His mother would need money, even if she were in a hospital. He jammed the bills into his jacket pocket before carefully replacing the volume.

Rummaging in the desk, Henry found a letter from his father with a Winnipeg return address. He stuffed it into his book bag. There was only one other thing he needed.

Going to the mantle over the stone fireplace, Henry took down the photograph of his father. Removing the picture from its small silver frame, he gently touched his father's black and white face, brushed away a speck of dirt and tucked the picture into his jacket along with the money.

He hadn't wanted his pa to leave and had begged to go with him, but his pa said Henry was too young. Maybe now, when Henry showed up ready to work like any able-bodied man, his father would change his mind.

He smiled and patted his book bag. He was through with his mother's rules and the endless babysitting, and he'd never have to worry about drowning in Nova Scotia.

This was not how he'd imagined today would go, but he wouldn't let anyone, not even his mother, tell him what to do. Like his hero, Tom Sawyer, Henry would seek his fame and fortune in the wide world. Maybe he couldn't hitch a ride on a Mississippi riverboat, but he could take a page out of Tom's book and live by his wits and by his own rules.

CHAPTER 3

2/10

Winnipeg had seemed much closer when they'd taken the family car. Henry kicked a stone as he trudged along, listening to the insects humming around him in the warm June night. But now there was no stupid car, and he was walking down the stupid road in the middle of the stupid night!

The full moon turned the trees to shimmering silver in the gentle breeze. As he passed farm after farm, he noticed hobo signs on several gateposts. One looked like a lightning bolt, and Henry copied the zigzag line into his journal with a note that it meant the house must have been struck by lightning.

He was tired and wondering how much farther it was to Winnipeg when a worn-out farm truck rattled to a stop beside him. The rust bucket was in sad shape, and there were two scrawny cows in the back, which didn't add to the appeal of the ride. It smelled strongly of manure, and Henry tried not to breathe through his nose.

"Where you headed, young fella?" the driver, a scarecrow of a man, asked as Henry climbed in.

Henry had thought of a believable story to explain why he was on the road at night alone. "My pa sent me home with money for my mother, and now I'm going back to Winnipeg to help him on his job."

This immediately aroused the driver's interest. "Your pa has work? I don't suppose the company he's working for is looking to hire another man? After I sell these heifers, I'll be looking for work myself. I'm hoping for six dollars a head. That'll carry my family for the rest of the month, but then we'll be needing more money."

Henry felt cornered. "Ah, actually, this is his last week, and then we're going to find other jobs so we can send more money home."

This seemed to surprise the man. "Well, if that don't beat all. Your pa has a real positive outlook on life. I've been looking for any kind of work and I can't find anything, not even sweeping sidewalks or digging ditches." He glanced furtively at Henry. "How you planning on living until your pa gets more work? The police don't take kindly to vagrants—folks with no money and no place to live. Why, they throw those poor souls right in jail."

"Oh, I'm no vagrant," Henry said proudly. "I have five dollars cash money."

"Five dollars! You're rich, son. I should warn you; there are a lot of ruffians out there who would rob you blind. Do you have your money stashed someplace safe?"

Henry patted his jacket pocket. "Yes sir,

I sure do." Feeling like a man of the world, he sat back to enjoy the ride. The miles bumped by and, exhausted from his long night, he soon drifted into a doze.

Henry was startled awake by a hand in his pocket. The truck was parked on the side of the road, and he could smell the farmer's rank breath. "Hey, what are you doing, mister?"

The man's eyes were wild. "My family's starving and I ain't got nothing but these measly cows to sell. I need that money!" He made a lunge for Henry.

"No! You can't have it!" Henry struck out with his fists, punching the man in the face with all his strength.

The man recoiled, cursing. "I'm gonna tear you up, kid!"

Grabbing his bag, Henry threw open the door and bolted into the trees at the side of the road. He slipped into the undergrowth and hid until the farmer grew tired of searching for him. As he watched the taillights of the truck disappear into the night, Henry still couldn't believe the man had tried to rob him. He had seemed so friendly.

Henry didn't feel safe until the sun came up and he saw a sign on the road that said *Welcome to Winnipeg.*

Winnipeg was a big place, but Henry didn't want to waste any of his precious money on streetcars. After getting lost several times and having to ask directions from impatient strangers, he finally found the boarding house where his father was staying. His pa would be so glad to see him, Henry was sure they'd go out for a big steak dinner to celebrate!

He walked up the broken wooden steps and knocked on the door. The sun was hot, and he desperately wanted a drink of water. His father would have water to give him—cool, clear water. At last a white-haired woman opened the door.

"I don't have any spare food, so move along," she snapped.

She was about to slam the door when Henry blurted out, "I don't want food.

I'm looking for my father, Michael Dafoe. He's staying here."

The old woman hesitated, frowning. "Never heard of him." She started to close the door again.

Henry pulled the picture out and held it up. "This is my pa. His letter said he's staying here and that he was going to work on the Glenmore Dam and Reservoir Relief Project."

The woman peered at the picture. "We're not big on names around here. There's no need. No one stays long enough to bother. Your pa was here, but he left about a month ago."

Henry felt a crushing wave of disappointment, followed by a flash of fear as he realized what this meant. He was alone in a strange city. What would he do now? "Did he say where he was going?"

"No, he didn't." The woman waved her bony hand dismissively. "They come and they go."

"Can you at least tell me how to get to the Glenmore Dam project?" Henry waited as patiently as possible, but patience wasn't one of his strengths.

"Never heard of it, sonny. Try the Canadian Pacific Railway yards. That's where all the men go to get jobs." She pointed. "Head west. You can't miss it."

The woman shut the door, and Henry stood staring at the weathered wood. The paint was peeling and the door was in serious need of repair. It occurred to Henry that if his father should return, it would be a good idea to let him know that Henry was looking for him. He felt around in his book bag and pulled out the stub of a red crayon. He looked at it and thought of Anne. Red was her favorite color. At the bottom of the door, he drew a small smiling face and, beside it, a letter *H* with an exclamation point. That was how Henry had signed notes to his father back home. Stuffing the crayon into his jacket pocket, Henry looked at what he had drawn. It was very much like a hobo sign. His father had been right. It was a great way of communicating.

This was not how he'd imagined today would go, but he was sure he'd find his father at the train yard and everything would be fine. Henry turned and started down the battered steps.

CHAPTER 4

When Henry arrived at the railway yards, there was a large crowd of men milling about. Some carried signs demanding jobs, others shouted that they didn't want to go on the dole.

Henry's father had told him about the dole. It was money the government gave you when your family was starving. Henry knew it was a shameful thing, something to be avoided at all costs. His pa said a real man earned his living by honest hard work and didn't take charity from anyone, which was why he'd left home to look for a job.

Past the tall fence, Henry saw the

big yard. The trains were amazing! He watched the donkey engines push and pull boxcars and even full-sized locomotives around the crisscrossing tracks. There was a huge roundhouse with tracks running into it from different directions. As Henry stared in fascination, a large engine, belching steam like a lumbering dragon, rumbled into the building. The engine stopped on a wide pivoting platform, which began to turn. When it came to a halt, the locomotive chugged off in a different direction.

Tearing himself away, Henry moved into the crowd. He felt uneasy as he searched for his father. He couldn't see him anywhere, and these men were very angry. They began to shout and to shove the train-yard gate. Someone threw a rock over the fence. Another man stepped in front of a big black car as it drove up. The car stopped, and within seconds the men were crowding around. The shouting became much louder as the mob rocked the car back and forth.

Two men standing in front of Henry backed away.

"Come on, let's get out of here!" the taller of the two said. "We'll go to the hobo jungle, where it's safe."

The other man laughed at this but followed his friend.

Henry was afraid a riot was going to break out. The tall man had said the hobo jungle was safe. Henry didn't know what a hobo jungle was, but it had to be better than this shouting, pushing, shoving throng of furious men.

He squeezed through the mob and followed the two strangers.

They made their way through a maze of streets until they reached the outskirts of the city. The sun had gone down, and in the gloom Henry could smell wood smoke drifting on the breeze.

He stopped. In the trees ahead of him were dozens of small campfires, ramshackle sheds and flimsy lean-tos. Shadowy men in tattered coats tended pots hung over the fires or sat huddled together, muttering to one another. Their unshaven faces looked sinister in the flickering light.

Henry swallowed. If this was the hobo jungle, he wasn't sure he wanted anything to do with it. It didn't look safe at all, but going back was out of the question. He didn't have anyplace to stay in the city. Had his father ended up here, with these dangerous-looking men?

Henry spotted an old canvas tarp lying on top of a pile of broken posts. If he were Tom Sawyer, or even Tom's best friend, Huck Finn, he'd take that tarp and make a teepee to live in while he was lost in the wilderness.

Henry inched behind the woodpile and pulled out a couple of sturdy pieces, then dragged the tarp and the wood into the trees. Wrestling with the posts, he wedged them into the ground a few feet apart and hung the tarp across. It wasn't like the teepees he'd seen in books, but it would do.

Crawling inside, Henry wrinkled his nose at the moldy smell. He rummaged in his book bag for the bread, meat and cheese he'd brought. Tearing off a small portion of each, he carefully wrapped up the rest and put it back in his bag. Since there was no telling how long it would be until he could get more food, he would have to ration the little he had left.

When Henry finished his meager meal, he plumped up the lumpy book bag to use as a pillow. He wished he'd brought a blanket with him. The temperature was dropping and the ground felt damp.

This was not how he'd imagined today would go, but at least wild animals wouldn't eat him while he slept. He was tired, scared, cold, hungry and thirsty. Henry curled up into a ball, pulled his coat around him against the night chill and fell asleep.

CHAPTER 5

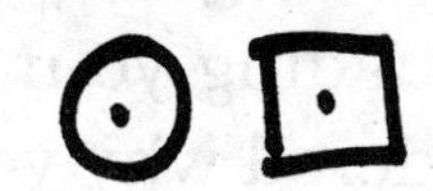

In his dream, Henry was stuffing himself with huge piles of freshly fried fish, bowls of fluffy mashed potatoes and basket-loads of biscuits and gravy.

With a jolt, he awoke and took a deep sniff. It wasn't a dream. He could smell fish frying.

Scrambling out of his makeshift tent, Henry blinked as the morning sunlight blinded him. When his watering eyes cleared, he looked around in amazement. Everything looked different. Instead of gangs of dangerous characters huddled over smoky campfires, the hobo jungle was filled with bustling men, laughing and cooking or shaking out blankets as they straightened the camp.

"Feel like a little breakfast?"

Henry spun around. A tall skinny man with a bushy beard grinned at him.

"I saw you building your campsite last night and wondered why you never came to join us for a cup of joe. I thought the neighborly thing to do would be to invite you to share the morning fry-up."

Henry didn't know whether to run or accept the hobo's offer. Then his stomach made a loud growling sound, and he decided he would eat now, run later. "I am a tiny bit hungry. I'll join you for breakfast, mister."

"The name's Fred Glass," the man said as he stuck out his hand.

Henry gingerly shook hands with Fred, whose clothes were more than a little shabby. "Mine's Henry Dafoe."

They sat around the fire, and Henry watched as several other men came by, holding out bowls or plates into which one of the golden fish was placed. Finally,

Fred held one up for Henry. "Courtesy of Light Fingers Flynn."

"Ah, I seem to have misplaced my plate." Henry pretended to search in his book bag. "And my fork, knife and spoon are gone too."

Fred smiled knowingly. "Well, lad, today's your lucky day. I happen to have a couple of extras. You keep 'em." He handed Henry a spoon and then expertly flipped the fish into a wooden bowl.

Maybe it was because he was so hungry or maybe it was because of Fred's cooking skills, but Henry had never tasted anything so delicious as that fish. He ate it down to the bones.

After breakfast, Henry thought it was a good time to show Fred his father's picture. "I'm looking for my pa. Have you seen him?" He held up the snapshot.

Fred shook his head. "You should talk to Clickety Clack." He pointed at a lean-to on the far side of the site. "Sooner or later, every man on the road comes through this camp. If your pa's a traveler, he'd have

bunked here a night or two and Clickety Clack would know. Heck, he knows everyone and everything that happens in the jungle, but be warned, that old cuss doesn't like youngsters—or anyone else for that matter." He chuckled.

Henry nodded his thanks and started across the camp.

Clickety Clack turned out to be an old man wearing a voluminous raggedy coat, purple plaid vest, tweed pants and long green striped scarf with a fringe on the bottom. The wispy gray hair sticking out from under his battered felt hat looked like it hadn't seen a comb in a long time, and the man's scruffy beard would have made Henry's mother frown. She would have called him grizzled. Henry thought he was disgusting.

"What do you want?" the old man growled as Henry walked up.

Henry held out his father's picture. "My name's Henry Dafoe, and I was wondering when this man came through here?"

The hobo screwed up his face and spat

a wad of chewing tobacco into the dirt at Henry's feet. "Never did."

This wasn't what Henry wanted to hear. "Are you sure, mister? His name is Michael Dafoe. Could you look again?"

"Are you deaf, boy? I said he was never here." The old man spat again, then started rolling up a well-used blanket.

Henry felt anger welling up inside him. What did this old coot know anyway? He looked around at the sprawling hobo jungle. "Just because you never saw him doesn't mean he wasn't here. You could have missed him. My father came here to work on the Glenmore Dam and Reservoir Relief Project, and I intend to find him."

The old hobo looked at him with stone gray eyes. "Did you say the Glenmore Dam Project?"

"Yes, that's right," Henry said with confidence. "He's there right now!"

Clickety Clack shook his head. "Young pup. You don't know a dang thing."

"I don't have time for this, old man."

Henry had never been much good at controlling his temper, and he was getting desperate.

Clickety Clack coughed—a wet, gooey sound. "Let me finish tying up my old turkey here and maybe I'll tell you something about the Glenmore Dam Project." The tramp calmly went back to rolling his blanket and securing it with a worn belt.

Henry's limited patience was gone and his temper fast taking over. Finally Clickety Clack stood and stretched his back lazily.

"Well now, if you're headin' to the Glenmore Dam, you're a might east of where you want to be." Clickety Clack's lip twisted into a crooked half smile. His teeth were stained yellow.

Henry wished he had a big stick so he could poke the aggravating old derelict. "How far? One block, ten blocks, a mile?"

Clickety Clack looked to the west as though he could see the dam right up the road. "Oh, a little farther than that."

The hobo paused again. Henry was about to blow a gasket.

Clickety Clack went on in his slow, aggravating way. “Not a block...not a mile...” He scratched absently under his arm. “More like two...*provinces.*”

Henry didn’t understand. “What?”

“You need to head two provinces to the west, boy. The Glenmore Dam is in Calgary, *Alberta.* It’ll probably take you a while, especially as I don’t think you’ve ever ridden the rods before.”

Henry swallowed. Alberta! His parents had never said anything about his father leaving Manitoba. One thing was certain; he wasn’t going to let Clickety Clack know how shocked and scared he was. No sir. He’d do what Tom or Huck would do. He’d find a way to get there by himself.

“Of course I’ve ridden the rods,” he blustered, not knowing what the rods were, let alone how to ride them. “It’s been a while, that’s all.”

“Is that a fact?” The hobo stuck a fresh plug of chewing tobacco in his cheek.

Henry felt a little foolish, but it was too late now. "I used to ride all the time, but that was ages ago, when I was just a kid. Remind me again how it's done?"

Clickety Clack roared with laughter, almost spewing his tobacco into the dirt. "You forget, do you? Well now, don't that beat all. You plan on hopping a freight to Calgary? Because that's about the only way a pup like you is going to make it out there. I was thinking of heading to Calgary myself, but I have to plan for it. It's a long way."

Henry knew the jig was up. "So what would it cost for you to take me with you?"

Clickety Clack spat a new gob into the dirt. "I travel alone, boy." A greedy gleam came into his eye. "But for curiosity's sake, what do you have?"

Henry thought of the five one-dollar bills in his pocket. He also remembered the desperate farmer who'd tried to rob him. He wasn't going to trust this old man for a minute. "I'll pay you five dollars *cash* to take me to Calgary." The mention of money immediately got the tramp's attention.

"You have that much on you? Where you hiding it?" Clickety Clack's hungry eyes went to Henry's book bag.

"All you need to know is that I won't pay until we get to the Glenmore Dam." Henry stuck his chin out defiantly. He wouldn't be tricked again.

"That's a long way to go on faith, boy. I'll have to see it before I take a step." Clickety Clack clasped his hands as though praying.

Hesitantly, Henry pulled the cash out of his pocket for the hobo's inspection.

Clickety Clack reached out a gnarled hand, but Henry snatched the bills back. "Is it a deal?"

The hobo rubbed his bristly chin. "Deal!" He grinned, then spat into his dirty palm and held it out for Henry to shake.

Reluctantly, Henry clasped the hobo's disgusting hand to seal the bargain.

This was not how he'd imagined today would go. He'd thought by tonight he'd be eating dinner with his father, but instead it looked like he'd be with this raggedy tramp, hopping a freight train to Alberta!

CHAPTER 6

"Okay, boy, this is where we catch our ride. As soon as I spot a train heading for Alberta, we wait for it to start rolling, then it's *all aboard.*" Clickety Clack stuck a fresh plug of tobacco in his mouth and settled in to wait.

They'd managed to sneak through a hole in the fence at the railway yards and were hiding near the tracks. It was well after noon, but the June sun was still a blistering ball in the clear blue sky.

"And how do you know which train is going to Alberta?" Henry asked his gruff guide.

Clickety Clack winked at Henry. "That's why you're paying me the big bucks, boy." Several trains went by but the hobo ignored them.

Bored with the endless waiting, Henry absently reached into his pocket and felt something wedged in the bottom. He pulled out the stub of red crayon he'd used to leave the hobo sign for his pa. As he doodled on the fence, he saw that his drawing resembled a locomotive. Henry blinked.

Why, he'd created a hobo sign! This one would let other boys know they could catch a train here. Henry wondered if there were any other boys in the world having adventures like his.

Clickety Clack glanced at Henry's drawing, narrowed his eyes and grunted.

Henry watched the engines pull into the yard, then slow to a stop with a loud whoosh and a huge cloud of billowing steam. He wondered if they were ever going to find a train bound for Alberta. "Which one are we going to take?" he asked impatiently.

A noise from the far side of a stationary boxcar made Clickety Clack grab Henry's arm. "Hush up, boy!"

"What's wrong?" Henry asked.

"Quiet! Over there, behind that boxcar—*bulls.*" Clickety Clack crouched even lower behind the large wooden crate they'd been using for cover.

Henry couldn't imagine why livestock would be roaming loose in a train yard, but when he stood to get a better look, Clickety Clack yanked him down.

"Didn't you hear me? I said there are two bulls behind that car and they've got a dog. Do you want us to get our heads busted open?"

The alarm in the hobo's voice alerted Henry to the seriousness of the situation. "We're not talking about cattle, are we?"

Clickety Clack shook his head. "No, fool! I'm talking about the meanest, toughest, worst kind of two-legged critter that ever walked the earth—railway police. Why, those guards would as soon crack your skull as give you the time of day. If they catch us, we're dead meat. We've got to hide."

Henry glanced around. "Hide? Where?"

Clickety Clack spat out a messy glob of greenish brown ooze. "Over there, in that water tank. The dog can't track our scent once we're in the water. Come on!" Clickety Clack made a dash for the tall wooden tower.

Henry followed reluctantly, fear making his feet drag. Did the old man really expect him to climb inside this huge vat and hang there like a rat in a water bucket?

"Come on, I'll give you a leg up onto the ladder." Clickety Clack made a cradle out of his hands and lowered himself so Henry could get a boost.

"I—I don't want to," Henry stammered, taking a step backward.

The hobo frowned, then rubbed his whiskers. "Oh, I get it. You can't swim. Don't worry, boy. I can't swim a stroke either, but we won't be in for long and we can hang on to the top."

Henry clenched his teeth. "No. I won't do it."

The hobo clambered onto the ladder that ran up the side of the water tank. "I'm telling you, it ain't safe out here. Now come on before you get us both beat up." He scrambled up the rungs with surprising speed and disappeared over the edge.

Henry looked behind him. The guards were almost at the end of the boxcar nearest him. He had to hide, but not in that water-filled casket!

He sprinted for a tall stack of crates at the end of the narrow alley between the rows of cars. Darting behind the wooden boxes, he ducked as two burly railway policemen rounded the end of the freight car. With them was a huge dog with a hungry gleam in its beady black eyes.

Henry's breath caught when he saw the vicious-looking beast. As the guards passed the crate where Henry and Clickety Clack had been hiding seconds before, the big dog stopped.

Its nose dropped to the ground. It sniffed a couple of times, then lifted its huge head to stare at where Henry was hiding.

Henry edged farther away as the dog padded toward him. He increased his speed as the two guards followed the dog.

Ducking under a boxcar, Henry ran to the next set of tracks and squeezed between two more cars. He snatched a look over his shoulder. Having caught his scent, the animal was now loping after him, foam-flecked drool sliding in slimy trails out of its massive jaws.

Henry sprinted to the edge of the train yard and came up against the high fence that he and Clickety Clack had found their way through earlier. Turning, he saw the animal closing on him. There was nowhere to run, nowhere to hide! Frantically, he dug through his book bag. His fingers closed around the remains of his food.

He tore off a piece of cheese and tossed it on the ground. The dog halted its

headlong attack, sniffed the tidbit and then slopped it up. Henry held out the rest of his food. The dog stopped, lifted one paw off the ground and whiffled the air.

"Nice doggy," Henry murmured. "Good boy, you want a tasty treat?"

The dog stepped closer. Henry waved the snack invitingly. "Then go get it!" He threw the food as far as he could, then sprinted in the opposite direction. As he crawled under a boxcar, he heard the dog scramble after his lunch. He also saw the two policemen running to where he'd been only seconds before.

Henry raced to the water tower. "Clickety Clack!" he called in a loud whisper. The old hobo's head peered over the edge of the tank. "Come on! We've got to make a run for it! The dog thinks I'm a lunch wagon, and he'll bring his two buddies with him."

Clickety Clack was out of the water and down the ladder in a twinkling. "Come on, boy. We've got a train to catch!"

Squelching with every step, Clickety Clack headed toward an engine that was making its way out of the big train yard, a long parade of boxcars in tow. "Do exactly what I do and keep your feet away from the rails!" he yelled as he ran alongside the slowly moving train.

Henry's heart pounded as the powerful steam engine shook the ground.

An open boxcar drew up alongside Clickety Clack. He tossed his bedroll in through the opening, then grabbed hold of the door edge and leapt aboard. "Jump!"

Henry looked behind him. The two policemen and the huge guard dog were closing in. The dog bared its teeth and snapped its powerful jaws as it tore after them.

Reaching up as he ran, Henry's fingers were only inches from Clickety Clack's outstretched arm as the train pulled away. In a last desperate effort, Henry lunged forward and clasped the hobo's hand, and with a mighty heave, Clickety Clack yanked him through the open door.

They were safe!

Henry lay sprawled on the dusty wooden floor, gasping.

Clickety Clack pulled himself to his feet and spat out the open door as he waved goodbye to the posse that had been chasing them. "So long, suckers!"

Henry sighed with relief. He felt the train vibrating beneath him in a steady rhythm as it carried them west.

This was not how he'd imagined today would go, but soon he would be with his father in Alberta, and vicious dogs, angry policemen and leaping aboard moving boxcars would all be behind him.

CHAPTER 7

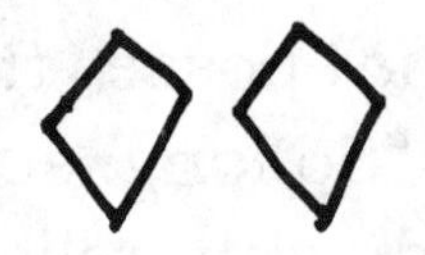

Lulled by the constant swaying of the train as it carried them west into Saskatchewan, Henry imagined he was on a riverboat. The steel rails were his river, and the boxcar his paddle wheeler. He was steaming down the Mississippi, just like his hero, Tom Sawyer. Life was grand!

Henry thought about writing Anne her very first letter, then decided she could wait and pulled his novel out instead. He sat at the edge of the door, rereading a favorite chapter of Tom's adventures, but his attention was drawn to the miles of parched fields he was traveling through.

He remembered his teacher talking about John Palliser's Triangle, which stretched across much of southern Alberta, Saskatchewan and into parts of Manitoba. The Triangle had dry sandy soil, no trees, and grassland that spread out to the horizon. In his mind's eye he could see a vast ocean of gently waving prairie grass, but now, in the searing heat of a drought, all that was left was burnt scrub and swirling dust devils.

Clickety Clack snored loudly as he slept on the boxcar floor. Henry looked around his temporary transport. The dusty wooden freight car was old and smelled of oil. It was not a place he wanted to spend much time in, that was certain.

He went back to watching the world pass by, mesmerized by the landscape.

Groaning loudly, Clickety Clack roused himself from his afternoon nap. "Well now, I'd say we need a little snack. I'm feeling a might peckish. Where's my old turkey?" He groped around for his bedroll, which had served as a pillow while he slept. "Let's have a look." Out of the rolled-up blanket came an assortment of food including a couple of squashed buns, a piece of beef jerky and two hard-boiled eggs.

Henry's stomach rumbled.

Clickety Clack laid out the feast on an old handkerchief that had materialized from one of his pockets. It was then that Henry realized why the hobo had so many pockets. He was wearing two coats, one over top of the other!

The tramp looked at him. "Where's your grub, boy? We'll eat now and go to the bread line in Regina when we get there tonight."

Henry sighed. "I had to feed it to the guard dog to get away."

Clickety Clack stared at him. "You gave *all* your food to that hairy beast? Why didn't you throw part of it and keep some for yourself? Kind of shortsighted, wouldn't you say, boy?"

Henry's temper flared. "I didn't know I was going to have to run for my life or I might have been more prepared. No one told me about the railway bulls and their boy-eating dog."

"And if you'd done what I said in the first place and climbed into that water tower, you could have kept all your food and still escaped." Clickety Clack tapped the shell of his hard-boiled egg with a jackknife that had magically appeared; he then pulled a tiny tin of salt out of yet another pocket. "Too bad, but I don't have enough to feed you and me both. I guess you'll have to wait till tonight." He peeled the egg and sprinkled it liberally with salt before greedily chomping into it.

"Fine with me! I'm not hungry anyway." Henry's stomach was gnawing on his backbone, but he wasn't going to beg for food. Not him! He went back to reading his book.

The elderly traveler continued to enjoy his meal. Henry swallowed; his mouth wouldn't stop watering. He knew he shouldn't look, but his eyes were drawn to the food.

Clickety Clack glanced at him from

under bushy gray eyebrows. “Oh, stop looking like the pigs ate your granny, boy. I reckon there’s enough here for two.” He tossed Henry an egg, followed by a bun and a sizable chunk of the jerky.

Henry tried to look as though he didn’t care one way or the other. “I guess I could force it down.”

They ate in silence while the miles slipped by in the lazy summer sunshine. A smudge on the horizon caught Henry’s eye, and he wondered what kind of dust storm it was. “There’s a strange...” he began.

“Be quiet!” Clickety Clack looked up, listening intently.

Then Henry heard it. A strange whirring sound filled the air.

“We’re in for it now!” Scrambling to his feet, Clickety Clack hurried to the open door and tugged at it.

At that moment, Henry saw them.

Millions and millions of grasshoppers!

With a hailstone rattle, the flying bugs hit the sides of the boxcar, plastering it with their slimy green bodies. The noise was deafening. Henry ran to help close the door. The grasshoppers smashed into his hair and face. He opened his mouth to yell, but his voice was drowned as insects filled his nose and throat. He couldn't breathe, and panic gripped him as his mind flashed back to that terrifying day at the creek when he had almost died.

He spat out the loathsome bugs and pulled on the door. It was jammed.

Henry could see that the bottom track was plugged with dead grasshoppers. He dropped to his knees and frantically dug the gooey green mush out of the track.

Clickety Clack heaved on the door, slamming it shut against the terrible storm. "This is not good. These little critters can strip a crop to the ground in minutes and drive cattle so wild that they stampede into fences."

Henry's head came up. "Feel that? The train's slowing down!" The car began to shudder. Then a horrible stench made his lunch rise in his throat. He clamped

his hand over his nose. "What's that awful stink?"

Clickety Clack shook off several grasshoppers that clung to his coat. "The wheels have squashed so many hoppers, we can smell the hot, oozing bug juice, and the reason we're slowing down is because as the critters get ground up, the steel wheels lose traction on the slimy rails. They act like grasshopper grease." He shook his head. "I've got a bad feeling about this."

As they waited, the sound of the laboring engine could be heard clearly above the drumming of the insects. Finally the train came to a complete stop, and the noise of bug bodies pounding into the boxcar gradually died away. Henry looked at Clickety Clack. "What's happening?"

"Nothing good for us," the tramp answered as the train jolted forward and backward along the slick tracks. Finally the jerking motions stopped and the air grew ominously quiet.

With the squeal of straining steel, Henry

heard the engine start chugging again, slowly at first, then faster. He sighed with relief.

This was not how he'd imagined today would go, but by tonight they'd be in Regina. Halfway to Calgary, halfway to finding his father. He braced himself for the hard snap that would come as their car rumbled into motion, but nothing happened. As Henry listened, the sound of the engine pulling away was distinct and frightening.

CHAPTER 8

“Grab your gear, boy. This is where we get off.” Clickety Clack slung the belt holding his bedroll over his shoulder.

Henry was confused, but for once he did as he was told without argument. He knew if he was to survive, his best chance was to listen to the old hobo.

They shoved the door open. The world was sunny again.

Henry jumped down and looked around. Their car, along with a dozen others, was parked on a siding in the middle of the empty prairie. “The train left us! We’re stranded!” He heard the panic in his voice. “What are we going to do?”

Clickety Clack spat out a gob of tobacco juice, which looked a lot like the grass-hopper guts Henry had scooped out of the door track. “You’re too soft, boy. The old road was spoiled is all, but we’ve got feet, don’t we?” he scoffed. “We can walk to Regina. It can’t be more than two or three days away.”

Henry stared at him in disbelief. “Two or three days! Are you crazy?”

Clickety Clack shot him a hard look. “Hold your tongue, boy. I’ve never taken guff from anyone, especially not a wet-behind-the-ears kid.”

“And I’ve never been stuck in the middle of the bald prairie before! It’s, it’s...” Henry searched for the right word.

“Terrifying?” Clickety Clack added helpfully.

“Aggravating!” Henry groaned. “I was supposed to see my father tomorrow.”

Clickety Clack threw back his head and gave a great roar of a laugh. “Well now, that’s life, boy. It doesn’t always go the way we plan, but once you’re on this ride there's no getting off, so make the best of it."

He squinted into the distance as though getting his bearings. "We go that way." He nodded to the west. Pulling a piece of chalk out of one of his pockets, he jotted a sign on the fencepost at the end of the siding. It was a circle with an arrow jutting out of it, pointing in the direction he'd indicated. "This will help other folks who get stranded here so they won't end up as buzzard bait." He tucked the chalk away and started walking. "Come on, boy. We've got a ways to go, and it ain't going to get any cooler."

Despite the delay, Henry comforted himself by remembering that he'd already made it out of Manitoba and halfway across Saskatchewan, a feat anyone would be proud of.

His mouth felt as dry as the dust under his feet. Henry smiled. First chance he got, he'd write and tell Anne how he almost died of thirst in the great Canadian desert and how buzzards were circling, waiting for him to drop. That was a story worthy of Tom Sawyer, for sure.

As he trudged beside Clickety Clack, Henry looked around at the parched fields and stunted grass. "What a horrible chunk of dried-out dirt. Why would anyone want to live in this dustbowl?"

Clickety Clack stopped dead in his tracks. "You listen to me, boy. I don't want to hear you talk like that again. This land is our friend and you don't kick a friend when he's down. It's years of drought that have ruined this place. All it needs to get back on its feet is water. Water is the key, boy. When the rains come—" he swept his arm as though gathering the entire prairie to him "—it will be home to herds of wildlife and flocks of birds, and it will be the finest place on earth to raise a family. This land will grow grain and crops enough to feed the world."

Feeling thoroughly chastised, Henry looked at the countryside again, this time with fresh eyes, imagining this burnt-out land covered with lush green crops and filled with life.

In the vast stillness, he breathed in the clean sweet air and heard the haunting call of a hawk overhead. It was as if the land was holding its breath until the rains came back and it was transformed into the answer to every farmer's prayer.

"I never thought of it like that before." He gave the old hobo a sidelong glance. "Back there, when I was rude to you, I was, well, out of line."

Clickety Clack grunted and started ambling down the road again.

As they walked, the late afternoon gold in the sky turned to a fiery red that finally faded to deepest mauve.

When Henry was so tired he didn't think he could take another step, Clickety Clack stopped and rubbed his hands together.

"That's exactly what I was hoping for!" he exclaimed with a chuckle.

Henry glanced around. "I don't see anything."

"No, I don't suppose you would." Clickety

Clack folded his arms across his tattered coat. "Tell me what you do see."

Henry peered around him. "Well, empty fields mostly, a dry streambed, a rail fence and a gate with a post on either side. Other than that, not a heck of a lot."

Clickety Clack shook his head. "Young whippersnappers! Don't use the eyes God gave them. See that?" He nodded at the post nearest them.

"Yeah, so, it's a worn-out gatepost..." Henry wondered what the tramp was getting at. Maybe the heat had melted the old coot's brain. Then he saw it. "Wait a minute...that's a hobo sign!"

Henry examined the symbol on the gate, then took out his journal and jotted it down. "I've got a list of these, but this one's new to me." It was four straight lines stacked one over the other.

"Well, it's not new to me. That, my boy, is our dinner." Clickety Clack was in high spirits now. "Say, I thought you knew about the code."

"I do, sort of. Back home I'd see these drawings on fences and I'd note them in my journal. My pa said it was the hobo code for travelers."

Clickety Clack nodded. "So it is, boy. It's a secret language only we knights of the road can decipher. This particular symbol means a housewife will feed you for doing chores. Come on, lad, we're about to sing for our supper." He pulled out a battered pocket watch and glanced at it. "And I'd say our timing is about perfect." With that, Clickety Clack began whistling as he strolled up the long driveway to the farmhouse.

Once they got to the house, Henry started up the front steps, but Clickety Clack stopped him. "No, no, lad. We're humble travelers, down on our luck. We go to the back door—" he winked at Henry "—which is usually the one closest to the kitchen!"

They made their way to the back of the house, where Clickety Clack removed his hat, smoothed back his straggly hair, dusted off his pants and straightened his vest. Just before rapping on the door, he spat out his plug of tobacco. A large woman wearing a faded apron answered the knock.

"Excuse me, madam," he began in a soft voice, "but my grandson and I were stranded today and we're wondering if you have any chores that need doing in exchange for a bite of sup?"

The woman frowned at Clickety Clack, and Henry thought she was going to tell them to scram, when her gaze fell on him. He tried to look forlorn and starving, which wasn't at all hard to do.

"Well now, I could use some kindling split. You two gentlemen," she smiled sweetly at Henry, "can chop some wood while I fix you a nice supper. My family and I finished eating not five minutes ago, and we have lots of leftovers."

"We'd be happy to help out, ma'am." Clickety Clack smiled winningly at the woman and headed for the woodpile with Henry in tow. When they got to the stacked rounds, Henry plunked down on a fat stump and prepared to watch Clickety Clack.

"I think you have mistakenly taken my seat, boy." Clickety Clack looked at him indignantly.

Henry raised his eyebrows, first at the old hobo, then at the big pile of logs. "You're kidding. I've never split wood in my life!"

"Then it's about time you learned." Clickety Clack shooed him off the stump as he stuck a fresh plug of tobacco in his mouth. "It's a simple thing, boy. You pick up the axe and turn that big hunk of timber over there into little sticks of kindling, preferably without chopping off your own foot in the process. Keep a-going until I tell you to stop."

Taking a deep breath, Henry picked up the heavy axe.

Clickety Clack looked around as Henry set to work. "It looks like these here folks are some of the lucky ones." He nodded toward a small lean-to. "See that forge?

I'd say this fellow is a blacksmith. More folks are using horses these days, and horses always need horseshoes. He's probably kept mighty busy and no doubt charges a pretty penny for his services."

By the time Henry had chopped a respectable pile of kindling, the sun had disappeared, his arms ached and his back was on fire.

"That seems about right." Clickety Clack rose to his feet. "Now for our pay."

They walked to the house, where the ancient traveler knocked politely. He was wiping his brow with a red handkerchief when the woman opened the screen door.

She glanced at the kindling and smiled, then handed them two heaping plates of food. "You hard-working gents can sit under that tree by the toolshed, and I'll bring you a pitcher of cold lemonade."

Henry felt giddy when she mentioned the lemonade. He was more than thirsty; he was parched down to the soles of his dusty boots.

Clickety Clack tucked the handkerchief away with a flourish, then stretched out his back. "Thank you, ma'am. A cold drink would go down nicely after that strenuous workout."

"Oh, dear!" The farmwife looked alarmed. "You shouldn't have chopped so much in this heat! Maybe there are a couple of slices of rhubarb pie left. I'll bring those along too."

Clickety Clack smiled as they headed to the tree.

That night the old hobo let Henry use one of his coats for a bedroll. "You're a bit soft to sleep rough" was all he said as he handed the coat over.

"Much obliged," Henry replied, realizing he meant it. As he lay on his back, staring up at the night sky, Henry marveled at the millions of tiny lights strewn across the vast black velvet curtain overhead.

This was not how he'd imagined today would go, but then he remembered how the hobo signs had led them to a delicious meal. Now that was something!

CHAPTER 9

They were up early the next morning, and Henry felt much better about his adventure. Just like Tom and Huck, he was making his way in the wide world. Okay, he needed a little help from Clickety Clack, but he was going to find his father in Alberta! By now his mother must have read his note. He didn't want to worry her, but a life riding the rails beat one on a boat any day. And as for Anne, why, he'd write her a long letter just as soon as he had a quiet hour or two. The exciting tale of his adventures would be told for years to come, of that he was certain. He'd stay with his pa in Calgary and work on the dam, make some real money and see the whole wide world.

Henry and the old tramp continued down the long road, their shoes kicking up puffs of powder-fine dust.

"Are you sure this is the way to Regina?" Henry asked after they had been walking several hours.

"All roads lead to Rome," Clickety Clack said cryptically. "In these parts, you end up in Regina whether you want to or not. It's the capital, you know."

Henry shot him a dark look. "I'm not dumb."

"Then stop acting like it. I know where we're going. That's what you hired me for." The old hobo stuck a chaw in his mouth and ambled on.

They continued their trek, the searing heat from the sun beating down mercilessly on their heads. For the hundredth time, Henry wiped his brow and wished he had a hat.

As evening drew in, Clickety Clack appeared to be searching for something.

"Keep your eyes peeled for a tall gate with a carving of a wooden fish for a latch. My memory ain't what it used to be, but I'd swear the Fergusons' spread is right along this road."

Henry was tired and hungry but did as he was told. Then he spotted it. "Over there, in the trees."

Clickety Clack spat out a gob of juice. "That's the ticket, boy. This is where we'll bunk for the night." He started walking toward the gate, then stopped and rubbed the dust off the side of a stump near the fence. "You can add this to your dictionary of secret signs if you don't already have it."

Henry leaned over and saw a drawing that was a curved line like a smile with two small circles above it. "What's it mean?"

"It means we won't wake up with dew on our faces." Clickety Clack chuckled. "It's safe to sleep in the barn! We'll be resting on a bed of soft hay tonight, boy."

They made their way to the old barn, and when they went inside, sure enough, there was a bucket of fresh water on a table and, beside it, a box of beef jerky and biscuits.

"How did these folks know we were coming?" Henry hungrily bit off a piece of the jerky.

"Oh, they didn't. All of us on the road know the Fergusons' place. These kind folks leave provisions in case a couple of travelers drop by for the night. They're mighty nice. They've got a boy, Johnny, about your age. He's a good lad."

While they were eating the delicious food, Henry scratched the newest sign into his journal. "This is a good one to know. It's nice in here." He looked around approvingly at the snug barn.

Clickety Clack harrumphed, then reached over and took Henry's journal and pencil from him. He quickly sketched another of the signs and wrote something beside it, then handed it back to Henry. "This is an important one to know."

Henry read the words beside the symbol, two sets of circles arranged over each other. "Generous people." He smiled at Clickety Clack as he bit into his fourth biscuit. "I can't argue with that."

Although he was tired, sleep eluded Henry that night and he tossed and turned for a long time. Finally he propped himself up on one elbow. "Pssst! Are you asleep, Clickety Clack?"

"I was until a second ago," the old hobo growled.

"You must have been riding the rods for quite a spell," said Henry.

Clickety Clack sighed. "Since I was about your age, and that was a long time ago." His voice sounded sad and Henry wondered why. This life was full of excitement and strange new places. He loved it.

Clickety Clack put his arms behind his head. "It was a cold spring when my ma died. My pa had lit out years before, and her death left me alone. An old gent passing through helped me bury my mother. Then, since there was nothing to hold me, I left with him. That was the start of my life on the road. I've been from one side of this country to the other more times than I can count."

"Do you ever get lonely?" Henry asked.

"I've spent a month moseying around the Yukon, where I hardly saw a soul, and never felt lonely. I've also been in jam-packed cities and discovered that sometimes the loneliest place in the world is smack in the middle of a crowd. City folks bump into an old hobo like me on the street and pretend they don't see me. At least out here, everyone's in the same boat and we try to help each other as best we can."

Henry thought about life on the road. He had to admit it was a tiny bit lonely, but it was still better than being on a fishing boat. "How did you get the name Clickety Clack?" he asked.

The tramp laughed heartily. "Why, on the road, everyone's got a special name, boy. Usually other fellas give it to you because of something different about you or a special talent you have. I was fourteen when I got christened Clickety Clack. I was hopping a freight out of Vancouver, and that old steam engine was picking up speed. I caught sight of three big railway bulls hot on my heels and knew if I missed that train I was in trouble. By golly, I took two steps, jumped for my life and bingo! I was into that boxcar just like that." He snapped his grimy fingers. "The other guys in the car said I went from standing still to landing in that car in the time it takes the big engine wheels to go around once—clickety-clack. The name stuck."

"I wish I had a special name." Henry put his arms behind his head too. "*Henry* sounds so boring. What kind of a name is that for a knight of the road?"

"Oh, I have exactly the right name for you, boy." Clickety Clack chuckled. "*Henry* is what your mama called you, but out here it would be shortened to Hank. I believe I'll call you High-handed Hank because of the way you're always bossing people around and acting like the rest of the world isn't worth wasting one minute of your time on."

Henry sat up excitedly. "You mean it? I've got my own hobo name! It's like a hobo sign. Only adventurous fellas like us understand what it means. *High-handed Hank.*" He rolled the name around in his mouth to see how it tasted. It was wonderful!

He should write Anne and tell her about his official hobo name, but he was too tired. He'd draw the new signs and include them in his letter the very next day, he promised himself.

This was not how he'd imagined today would go, but the smile on his face didn't fade as he drifted off to sleep.

Chapter 10

The next morning, dawn was still stretching pale pink fingers into the eastern sky when they roused themselves from their sweetly scented beds. Before they left the barn, Clickety Clack reached into one of his many pockets and pulled out a scrap of paper and the stub of a pencil.

"What are you doing?" Henry asked.

"Basic courtesy, boy." Clickety Clack licked the end of the pencil and hastily scribbled a thank-you note. When he'd finished, he placed the paper beside the box where the biscuits had been.

Henry looked at the note, then rummaged in his book bag. He pulled out a small blue ball and placed it on the note. “It’s my never-miss metal marble shooter. I thought Johnny might like it.”

Clickety Clack patted him on the shoulder. “Now you’re getting the hang of this, Hank.”

Henry felt good as they headed out into the rosy morning light.

Several hot hours later they came to a fence with scrub pasture on the other side. Clickety Clack surveyed the barbed wire with disgust. “We have to cross this field. Stand on the bottom strand and pull up the top one, will you, Hank? I don’t bend like I used to.”

Henry did as he was told, and the hobo ducked through the fence. Clickety Clack adjusted his old turkey and began striding across the sparse pasture.

Henry pushed between two strands and winced as one of the sharp barbs bit into the skin on his arm, making a checkmark-shaped cut.

Running to catch up, Henry noticed piles of fresh manure scattered in the field and looked around for the cow that had left those calling cards. As he passed a small stand of trees, he saw movement in the shade.

"Clickety Clack, watch out!" Henry yelled, but it was too late.

With a thunderous bellow, a large black bull burst from the trees, its tail twitching like a deranged metronome.

Clickety Clack took one look, then gestured frantically. "Come on, Hank. Mr. Bull doesn't want company!"

Henry didn't need to be told twice. He sprinted for the fence.

Snorting angry gusts of fetid air, the bull lowered its massive head and turned on Henry, two sharp horns pointed directly at him like the sights of a gun.

Clickety Clack took off his hat and waved it. "Hey, you, pick on someone your own size! Here, Bossy, Bossy, Bossy!" The huge animal's attention veered toward him.

The bull pawed the dirt, throwing up clouds of choking dust; then with a roar it charged the old hobo.

Clickety Clack whirled and raced past Henry, reaching the fence in seconds. He grabbed a post with one hand, then leapt clear over the barbed wire. As he landed, his knees buckled and he rolled in the dirt.

Henry dove under the wire and slid to safety just as the furious animal stampeded past.

At first Henry felt relieved.

Then he sniffed. The aroma of rotten manure was overpowering.

He looked down and groaned. A dark brown smear ran down the full length of his shirt.

"Don't stand too close, Hank, you're making my eyes water!" Clickety Clack fanned the air with his hat as though that would clear the horrible smell, then grimaced and reached for his ankle.

"Clickety Clack! Are you okay?" Forgetting his own problem, Henry rushed over to him. The tramp's face was gray under its coating of dust, his eyes full of pain.

"I think I've twisted my ankle." He tried to stand. "It's no good, I can't put any weight on it."

"I can help." Henry ran to a tall poplar tree near the fence. A stout branch with a fork at one end lay on the ground. Picking it up, he hurried back to Clickety Clack. "Do you have your jackknife handy?" The hobo searched in his pockets and pulled out his knife. Henry whittled the branch until he had it trimmed the way he wanted. "Wrap the fork with a piece of cloth and you can lean on it."

Clickety Clack took off his scarf and wrapped it around the top of the branch, then grabbed the hand Henry offered and struggled to his feet. Leaning on his makeshift crutch, he tested it out. "Works fine! Good job, Hank." He stopped and sniffed. "No offence, but as a traveling companion, you stink!"

Henry grinned. "Think of it as prairie perfume."

They looked at each other, relieved to have escaped the angry bull, and then

Clickety Clack slapped Henry on the back and laughed his big-bellied laugh. "Whoo-eee! We were within a whisker of death, Hank, and that's the truth. I thought we were goners for sure!"

Henry felt a little giddy too. That bull must have weighed a ton. "Whoo-eee!" he crowed, trying to mimic the old man's gleeful exclamation. "I don't think I've ever run so fast. Not even when I stuck that garter snake down Constance O'Brian's back and her two older sisters came after me with a broom." He laughed along with the injured tramp.

"Come on, Hank, we've got miles to go before we rest." Clickety Clack gingerly tried a couple of steps.

"Give me one minute!" Henry ran to the fence and took the red crayon out of his bag. Hastily, he drew a picture of two big horns chasing a small stick figure.

"What in tarnation is that supposed to be?" Clickety Clack asked.

Henry tucked his crayon back in his bag. "It's my hobo sign to warn the next traveler that Mr. Bull owns this pasture."

The old tramp raised his bushy eyebrows. "Well, now, I ain't going to argue with you on that one. In fact, I think I'll add it to my own list of secret signs."

Together they made their way down the empty road into the late afternoon sun.

"I need to rest a bit," Clickety Clack said as he sat in the shade of a towering tree.

They'd been resting a lot more frequently and Henry was getting worried. The old man's skin was ashen. "Mind if I take a look at that ankle?" Henry asked.

The hobo gingerly pulled up his pant leg. The ankle was an alarming size, swollen and purplish black. Henry remembered seeing Old Man Wilson's leg; it had looked like that—right before they cut it off! "Maybe we should find a doctor."

Clickety Clack nodded as he struggled to his feet, and Henry moved beside him so he could lean on the boy's shoulder. They walked slowly on in silence.

"Not far now, Hank. Up there, see that house in the trees?" Clickety Clack used his crutch to point to a small white-washed house in a stand of poplars. "And the sign on that rock yonder?" He pointed to a big boulder. On the side was a cross with a circle containing a smiling face etched in the top right quarter. "That means a doctor lives here and he won't charge us for his services. Let's make a house call."

The young doctor had the whitest cleanest hands Henry had ever seen. He told them he was about to leave to deliver a baby, but when he saw Clickety Clack's ankle, he made the old man come in so that he could examine the injured limb.

"It's not broken, but that's about the worst sprain I've ever seen," he said as he bandaged the foot. "I'll be gone a couple of days, but there's a place for you to rest in the barn. You need to stay off that foot for a week." Before he left, he gave them food and apologized that he didn't have more.

"Not to worry, Doc. We'll get by, right, Hank?" Clickety Clack slapped Henry on the back. Henry smiled weakly.

As he scrubbed his manure-stained shirt at the pump outside, Henry thought about the doctor's words: No travel for a week! He had to find his father, and a week's delay wasn't in his plans.

When they went to the faded red barn, Henry was surprised to see one of the big stalls contained two canvas cots, a pot-bellied stove, chairs and a table with a kerosene lantern. "Looks like the doctor's used to houseguests, or should I say barn guests."

"I'll add this one to my list of great stops." Clickety Clack carefully lowered himself onto one of the cots. "Mighty fine," he sighed tiredly. "Mighty fine." In minutes, the exhausted hobo was snoring softly.

Sitting on the other bed, Henry took out his journal and tried to write the long-overdue letter to his sister, but only got as far as *Dear Anne.* He kept sneaking looks at Clickety Clack to make sure the old tramp was all right.

There was no reason he had to stay, Henry thought. He could go on without the old man. High-handed Hank could hop a freight, find food and end up in Calgary with or without Clickety Clack. He didn't owe the hobo anything. The agreement had been payment when they reached Calgary. Henry looked at the sleeping man. In a flash, he made up his mind. He would leave now, before Clickety Clack woke up. The doctor had left plenty of food, and the water bucket was full. Henry was pretty sure the old man could make it to the outhouse by himself. There was nothing holding him here.

This was not how he'd imagined today would go, but he'd learned a lot on the road and could take care of himself. He didn't need anyone's help. Gathering his belongings, Henry silently slipped out of the barn.

CHAPTER 11

After an hour slogging down the gravel road, Henry's thoughts turned to supper. He kept his eyes peeled for a welcoming sign on a gatepost. Once he found one, he would sing for his supper.

Henry whistled as he strolled. He was High-handed Hank, knight of the road, free to roam wherever adventure took him.

But his mind kept slipping back to Clickety Clack. He wondered if the injured hobo's ankle was any better and hoped the old geezer had been able to make it to the outhouse by himself.

After rounding another bend in the

endless road, Henry spied a faded hobo sign on a fencepost. This one was a flat-bottomed triangle with arms sticking out of two sides. He smiled. They looked like little hands held up in the air; maybe this family gave you two fists full of food.

Henry marched up to the back door and knocked firmly. A loud explosion made him whirl around. Terror seized him, rooting him to the spot. A grimy old man in filthy coveralls stood ten yards behind him, and he was holding a shotgun!

Henry could taste rock salt in the air.

"Get off my property before I blow you to kingdom come!" The angry man raised the weapon.

"S-s-sorry, mister!" Henry stuttered. "I was looking for a bite of sup...in exchange for me chopping some wood!"

"I don't feed bums and I chop my own wood. Now get a move on!" He pointed the gun into the air and fired again.

Henry lit out of there as fast as his legs could carry him. Once he hit the woods, he stopped to catch his breath and watched as the crazy man stomped back into his house.

This was not what he had signed on for! Being shot at was not fun. He skirted the edge of the trees, keeping the house in view.

It was then that he spied a treasure worth two fists full of gold.

Two fat pies sat cooling in the kitchen window. His mouth watered. What did a mean old man like that need with two pies?

Now Henry Dafoe, nice upstanding boy who went to church on Sundays and hardly ever cursed, would never steal. It was wrong and against all the rules.

But High-handed Hank, knight of the road, abided by no such rules.

Henry darted from tree to tree, then edged his way along the wall of the house until he was under the kitchen window. Reaching up, he took one of the pies and dashed for the woods. At any moment he expected to feel rock salt smack him in the behind.

Once in the sanctuary of the trees, he grinned. Tom and Huck would be proud of him. He was a prairie pirate of the first order, plundering ships laden with gold. He looked down at his treasure and sniffed the spicy apple aroma. He thought how much old Clickety Clack would love a big piece of apple pie.

A sharp flash of guilt ran through Henry as he remembered all the things Clickety Clack had done for him. He sighed. He had to go back. He couldn't leave the old guy alone; it wasn't right. So what if he found his father next week instead of tomorrow? With the precious pie cradled safely in his arms, Henry started walking back toward the doctor's faded red barn.

As Henry strolled into the barn, Clickety Clack was pouring a cup of the coffee he'd made on the potbellied stove. "Feel like a big slice of apple pie with that coffee?" Henry asked.

Clickety Clack looked up in surprise. "When I noticed your gear was gone, I wondered what had happened to you." His eyes looked sad, and Henry felt a fresh wave of guilt. Then the old man's expression changed. "But I see you've been out hunting the wild Canadian pie. Did you catch that one with a snare or a net?"

As they feasted on the best pie he'd ever tasted, Henry knew he'd done the right thing in coming back.

"So how did you come across this delicious masterpiece?" Clickety Clack asked after finishing his third slice.

Henry smiled. "It all started when I saw a hobo sign on a fencepost. I thought I'd go and offer my services in exchange for supper, like we did with that farm lady." He rubbed the back of his neck sheepishly. "But I must need reading glasses. The farmer chased me off with a shotgun."

At this, Clickety Clack gave him a startled glance. "What did this sign look like?" Henry described the triangle symbol and the old hobo burst out laughing. "You are one lucky boy, High-handed Hank.

That means a man with a gun lives there and he ain't afraid to use it. The best thing to do when you see one of those is to pass right on by. After seeing you write that sign for hopping a freight, it never occurred to me that you didn't know what the signs meant."

Henry looked surprised. "You mean I got it right and that's what the picture of a train means?"

"Of course that's what it means. That was why I thought you knew the code. Maybe I better have a look at that journal of yours in case you've got any more wrong."

Henry retrieved his journal and proudly showed Clickety Clack his list of signs and their meanings. The old man read the list, then shook his head. "Who told you what those symbols mean?"

"No one. I'm excellent with puzzles and figured them out on my own," Henry boasted.

"Well you figured these all wrong, High-handed Hank."

Henry was about to protest, but the disaster with the triangle sign was too fresh. He shrugged, a grin tugging at the corners of his mouth. "Maybe I do have a thing or two to learn about these particular puzzles."

Clickety Clack chuckled, then took out his pencil. "Now, let's set you straight..."

Henry was amazed. So many of his guesses had been dead wrong: the top hat meant that a wealthy gentleman lived at that house and had nothing to do with funerals, and the cat alerted you that a kind old lady lived there—no fighting cats anywhere! Clickety Clack showed Henry the symbols for food or good drinking water, where work was available and where hobos weren't welcome. There were symbols telling you where it was good to camp or that you were in a dangerous neighborhood.

When Clickety Clack saw the zigzag lightning bolt, he whistled. "You were lucky there too, son. That's one to be avoided. It means a vicious dog is waiting to take a bite out of your rump." He wrote the correct meanings beside the symbols and added a dozen more.

"It *is* like a secret language." Henry looked at the list, which now filled four pages.

"That it is, Hank," said Clickety Clack. "And it allows old hands like me to get by. The road is long for a man on the move."

The hobo had a faraway note in his voice that reminded Henry of the wind sighing in the empty prairie sky.

They were bunking down for the night when Henry noticed Clickety Clack's ankle seemed to be giving him less pain. "It looks like you might be healed up earlier than the doctor thought."

"Oh, that! We'll be on the road tomorrow. Doctors are always overprotective. I've done worse and didn't take any time at all to lick my wounds. I'll be fine tomorrow and we should be in Regina by nightfall."

As Henry wrapped himself in his blanket, he realized that he'd nearly left Clickety

Clack behind for nothing. They'd only lost one day and were rested and well fed because of it.

This was not how he'd imagined today would go, but as he fell asleep, he knew that loyalty was something he would never again take for granted.

CHAPTER 12

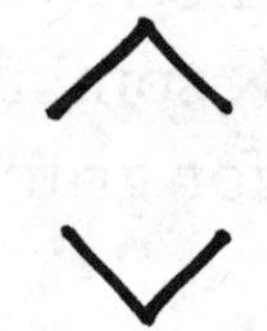

"At this rate, Hank, you'll be having supper with your pa tomorrow night!" Clickety Clack said as he and Henry strode down a busy street in Regina. They were on their way to the railway yard to catch a train to Calgary.

The old tramp stuck a fresh plug of tobacco in his mouth, then offered a chaw to Henry.

Henry didn't want to offend Clickety Clack, but the thought of chewing tobacco made him sick to his stomach. "No thanks! I'll stick to cigars."

Clickety Clack stopped in his tracks, momentarily taken aback, and then burst out laughing.

Henry joined in and found himself laughing so hard his sides hurt. "Hey, look there!" He pointed to a faded outline of a train engine. "We can catch the train here."

"Why, Hank, you got that exactly right! The bulls here are a good bunch and don't give us grief. There are lots of trains headed to Calgary, and one of those rolling hotels has a room with our name on it." Clickety Clack heaved himself over the fence.

Henry didn't like jumping onto moving boxcars, but he knew he had no choice. "I was wondering," he began as they threaded their way through the train yard, "when you talked about riding the rods, what exactly *are* they?"

Clickety Clack spat, expertly hitting an empty can on the ground. "That's one ride I hope you never have the privilege of taking." He pointed to the slender steel shafts that ran underneath the length of the boxcars. "See there. Those are the rods, and some poor devils wedge themselves up under a car and grab on to them for dear life while the train speeds on. In the winter, men freeze to death, and in the summer they become so hot and thirsty it's almost impossible to hang on. Not something you want to try. Up top's not much better." He pointed to the roofs of the cars. "You darn near choke to death in the tunnels when the engine's black smoke fills your lungs and you're breathing cinders. No, it's best to be inside a boxcar, but sometimes you don't have a choice, and then it's a dangerous ride."

Up ahead, a train started rolling, making the long string of cars jolt and bump. "Come on, Hank. That's our ride!" Clickety Clack hurried toward the slowly moving train. As they ran beside the train, a car with an open door drew alongside. Grabbing the edge of the door, Henry swung up onto the wooden floor. "I did it!" he shouted excitedly, then turned to see Clickety Clack falling back. With his bad leg, he couldn't run fast enough and in a minute the car would be past his reach.

"Give me your hand!" Henry yelled, holding on to the door rail as he reached for the old hobo. He could see the sweat running down Clickety Clack's face. The whistle blew and the train started picking up speed. Henry dropped to his stomach and stretched as far out as he could.

Clickety Clack lunged forward and clasped Henry's hand. The weight of the old man pulled on Henry's arm. Henry yanked with all his strength, refusing to let go, but he wasn't strong enough. He was being dragged out of the car.

Henry could see the big steel wheels below him and knew he was in trouble. They looked like huge metal meat grinders.

Suddenly, strong hands grabbed him, jerking him back inside while others hauled his friend aboard. Clickety Clack rolled onto the floor as Henry fell backward into a tall man standing behind him.

"You should have said something sooner. We didn't realize you were in trouble till you started sliding out of the car head-first."

Henry looked into the bearded face of Fred Glass. "Thanks, Mr. Glass! I'm mighty glad you decided to lend a hand." He remembered the meat-grinder wheels and swallowed.

"That was too gosh-darn-it close, Fred! Next time don't wait for a dang engraved invitation!" Clickety Clack grumbled as he dusted himself off.

Henry saw there were half a dozen other hobos in the car. They all looked hungry and tired, and their eyes had no light in them and certainly no laughter. Henry wondered what terrible troubles had extinguished the joy in their lives.

"You heading for Vancouver too, Clickety Clack?" Fred asked. "Me and the boys are going to pick fruit on the coast, maybe work on the docks."

Clickety Clack shook his head. "High-handed Hank," he jerked his thumb at

Henry, who grinned broadly, "and me, we're getting off in Calgary."

Henry picked up his bag and checked to make sure his precious book and journal were still safely tucked inside. "We're going to meet my pa. Clickety Clack says we'll be there tonight."

Fred stroked his beard. "I'd say right about time for supper at the mission. You haven't lost your touch, you old rod rider."

Clickety Clack harrumphed indignantly and slumped against the wall of the gently swaying car. Henry followed and tried to harrumph too, but it came out more of a cough.

The small band of travelers sat huddled in the dusty car, and soon a skinny fellow named Boxcar Charlie pulled out a harmonica. The sound was lonely and made Henry think of home. He wondered how his mother was doing in the special hospital and if his sister was having any trouble with the nuns at the convent. He felt bad about not writing to her.

"That was a near miss back there," Fred said, offering Henry a slice of bread and some cheese. "I once saw a fellow trying to hop a freight and timing it wrong. Well..." He looked down at the floor. "Let's just say he didn't make it."

Henry thought of those terrible hungry wheels and shuddered. The other men began to tell stories about riding the rails.

"My name's Whistlestop and I remember being stuffed under a car, hanging on to those blasted rods, during a winter run to Saskatoon. I darn near froze to death. Lost all the toes off one foot, and my eyelids froze to my cheeks. I had to wait till the train hit the station and the railway bulls pulled me off. They poured warm coffee on my face to thaw me out."

Even thinking about this made Henry shiver. The others joined in with similar harrowing stories.

"Once I was panhandling in a little place near Ottawa, and the police ran me out of town. They busted me up so bad, I still can't hear right in this ear." The toothless old man tapped the left side of his head.

Henry listened in openmouthed astonishment. This was a side of being on the road he hadn't thought about before.

The conversation shifted to work and companies they'd heard were hiring, then to how the government needed to create more jobs. Finally, as the miles churned by, the talk turned to home.

"I left my family on the East Coast, been trying to find work all across Canada. There are no jobs for the likes of us," said a shabby fellow who was missing two fingers on his left hand.

"My name's John and I ain't never ridden the freights before." John had skin like old leather. "Last year the hoppers got my crop, and before that, rust killed the wheat. This spring I used the last of our savings to buy seed, but the crop was burnt to a crisp by May."

A boy not much older than Henry spoke next. "I have seven younger brothers and sisters and figured my folks didn't need another mouth to feed. I'm nearly sixteen and man enough to take care of myself." The boy's voice was defiant, but Henry saw his lips quiver.

Looking at the gaunt faces, Henry realized with surprise that these men were not illiterate tramps who needed the hobo signs to get by; many were educated, and some had been schoolteachers or shopkeepers, but they had now lost everything. Henry felt sad for them. He knew how much his family's farm meant to his folks.

Henry pulled out his copy of *Tom Sawyer*, but somehow he didn't feel like reading about Tom and Huck. He leaned back and felt the wheels vibrating through the floor of the car. Mr. Glass had said they'd crossed the border and were in Alberta now. He was almost there.

This was not how he'd imagined today would go. Henry wondered what his life would be like riding the rails, never settling down in one place or having enough money to buy a meal. Being a prairie pirate was fun, but he suddenly wanted very much to see his family again.

CHAPTER 13

The evening sky was bruised purple when Clickety Clack nudged Henry awake. "Have a look at this, Hank."

Henry stretched his aching muscles. Sleeping on the hard wooden floor of a rocking boxcar was nothing like his soft bed at home. He followed Clickety Clack to the open door and looked out across the endless prairie.

Henry was awestruck. "Unbelievable!" To the west, rising out of the flat prairie, were the majestic Rocky Mountains!

They trailed across the horizon like a parade of tall sailing ships, their jagged masts reaching to the stars. Each towering peak glistened in the early evening light. Snow! They still had snow at those lofty elevations. Gently rolling hills spread out at their feet like a giant's rumpled carpet. Henry could imagine those hills covered by a vast golden ocean of grain, but now the fields were dry and empty.

All Henry could do was stare in open-mouthed wonder.

"The scenery's something, all right. Calgary's not far now." Clickety Clack looked around for his bedroll. "We'd best gather our belongings."

Henry eagerly grabbed his book bag and sat with his legs dangling over the edge of the door as the lights of Calgary flickered into view.

Calgary was a city much like Winnipeg. Tall buildings, short buildings, black cars rumbling past and people, lots of people. The city breathed with a life of its own.

Their traveling companions wished High-handed Hank and Clickety Clack good luck as the train pulled into the railway yard.

"Take care of yourself, Hank." Fred Glass extended his hand and Henry shook it.

Henry looked at the ragtag group and realized how close you could become in a short time. These men all faced hunger, loneliness, despair and the pain of being away from their families, but they had fed him, helped him and called him friend. It was strange to think they would go on with this nomad's life, using the secret signs to find food or a place to sleep.

"Thank you for making me feel so welcome." There was a catch in his voice. "I don't know if we'll ever meet again, but I hope each of you finds what you're looking for."

Henry and Clickety Clack jumped off the car and strolled into the fading evening light. After saying goodbye to the gang, Henry didn't feel much like talking.

They walked for a long time until Clickety Clack pointed to a worn-out store with a sign that read *Seventh Street Mission.* "Jackpot!" He spat into the gutter. In front of the building was a long line of men.

"What are they waiting for?" Henry asked curiously.

"Food," Clickety Clack said matter-of-factly. "That, Hank, is a bread line and this is a soup kitchen. It goes hand in hand with the dole. We'll get supper here and, if we play our cards right, a place to bunk for the night. Follow my lead..."

Henry remembered his father's words about the dole being a shameful thing and real men not taking charity, but here were many men accepting a hand-out. They couldn't all be freeloaders. These men were like his friends in the boxcar—good people temporarily caught in a bad place. Eating a free meal when you were starving didn't mean you were weak or lazy.

The old hobo and the young boy inched forward in the line. Finally they were inside, and Henry saw a counter on which sat a giant soup kettle and, beside it, dozens of neatly stacked loaves of bread.

Each man stepped up and held out his bowl. An extremely large woman with tinted spectacles stood behind the big black cauldron. She sucked her teeth as she carefully filled each bowl with steaming soup. A tiny lady with gleaming paper-white hair then gave each man a thick slice of bread. The large room was filled with long tables where the men sat and ate.

When Henry and Clickety Clack reached the soup woman, Henry held out his bowl.

Clickety Clack put his hand on Henry's slender shoulder. "This is my young grandson, ma'am, and we're much obliged for the meal. We've been on the road for weeks."

Henry felt a flush of guilt at the lie, but under the circumstances he was sure his mother would agree that stretching the truth a little was acceptable.

The portly woman nodded in understanding, then smiled sympathetically at Henry as she filled his bowl right to the brim. "You eat all that soup, young man. It's full of hearty vegetables."

Henry sniffed. It seemed those "hearty vegetables" were for the most part cabbage. He thought of how he used to complain about his mother's cabbage soup. Maybe he was hungrier or perhaps just wiser, but this time the soup smelled wonderful and Henry's mouth watered. He thanked her and moved to the bread lady.

"My my, son, you look half starved. I think you need two pieces." The bird-like bread lady added a second piece to Henry's bowl.

Henry bobbed his head and thanked her.

Clickety Clack continued talking. "Yes, he's been through a lot. He lost both his parents in a tragic accident." At this, Clickety Clack took off his old hat in a gesture of respect for the imaginary tragedy. "He's never been the same since."

The wily hobo lowered his voice so only the two ladies and Henry could hear. "He's mighty afraid to sleep outside, you know, because of his parents' misfortune...the grizzly bear..."

"Oh my! Oh my!" The bird lady's hands fluttered like wings in front of her face.

Henry did his best to look like an orphan. Shocked, the spectacled lady sucked on her teeth dramatically. "Land sakes! He shouldn't have to suffer any more than he already has." She crooked her finger at Clickety Clack, who moved closer. "Come by later and you and the boy can sleep in the back." She winked, then looked at Henry and shook her head sadly.

The hobo and the boy moved on.

"Well, now, I'd say that went rather well." Clickety Clack grinned as they sat at one of the tables.

"But what you told them wasn't true. My parents are both alive." Henry didn't like the idea of lying to old ladies.

"Look, boy, if I have a chance to sleep in a bed, I think it's worth a little white lie. No one was hurt and we don't have to huddle in a doorway tonight. There are worse things than grizzly bears in the big city. Now, eat your soup." He reached over and took half of Henry's second piece of bread. Henry raised an eyebrow and Clickety Clack scowled. "What are you gawking at? I'm half starved too, or didn't you notice?"

They loitered outside the kitchen until the last homeless man left, then slipped inside for a good night's rest.

In the mission's narrow back room, while Clickety Clack snored peacefully on one of the two hard beds, Henry rummaged in his book bag until he found his journal and the chewed stub of a pencil. Ever since he'd said goodbye to the other travelers, he'd been thinking of his mother. Before he could sleep, he had to write her. He wanted to let her know he was safe and that he was sorry for... well, for *everything*. He thought of the money he'd stolen. That had been wrong, he knew that now.

When he'd finished writing to his mother, he tore a fresh page out of his journal and wrote a special letter to Anne, using simple words and correct hobo signs to explain his adventures. Tomorrow he would buy an envelope and a three-cent stamp. His mind replayed everything he'd gone through, and he remembered how lonely he'd felt on the train, listening to the hobos' stories.

This was not how he'd imagined today would go, but he wanted his mother and Anne to know that he finally understood something very important—home and family mattered more than anything.

Chapter 14

The next morning they arrived at the Glenmore Dam and Reservoir Relief Project. Henry couldn't believe he'd made it. The odds had been against him, but he hadn't given up. Henry could have whooped out loud for joy! Tom and Huck would have been proud of him.

Henry couldn't pull his eyes away from the huge dam. It soared in a towering concrete wall to the far side of the gorge where, one day, water would back up and cover the entire valley spread out in front of him.

The site was a hive of activity. Men toiled with picks and shovels as wheelbarrows and horse-drawn wagons trundled among the work parties. Henry wondered how he was going to find his father in all this commotion.

"Let's go see the foreman. He'll tell us where your pa is." Clickety Clack started toward a small, corrugated metal building.

Once inside, Henry marched up to the desk and held out the picture of his father. "My name is Henry Dafoe and this is my father, Michael. He's working here. Can you tell me how to find him?"

Frowning, the foreman looked at the picture, and then recognition flooded his face. "Sure! Mike Dafoe. He's working down by the river." The foreman looked past Henry to where Clickety Clack stood in the doorway. "You looking for a job, buddy? This is your lucky day. I can use a man on shovel detail." He pushed a piece of paper across his desk. "Sign on the dotted line and report to the crew chief for assignment."

Clickety Clack hefted his bedroll and

shuffled his feet. “Much obliged, mister. Let me take the boy to his pa first.”

Henry and Clickety Clack walked to the edge of the high embankment over-looking the river. Henry smiled up at the old hobo who’d brought him so far and taught him so much. “This is a day to remember, Clickety Clack. A job on the dam for you and I’ll finally find my pa. Everything’s working out swell! My pa will want to meet you. You’ll like him and I know he’ll like you.” Henry couldn’t stop talking or smiling, but when he looked at Clickety Clack’s face his smile faded.

The hobo shook his head. “I don’t fit in here, Hank. This is no life for an old rod rider like me. I’ve got traveling dust in my shoes.”

“But I thought you were going to take a job here, with my pa and me.” Henry’s throat felt tight and his eyes swam. “Wait! The money I owe you!” He fumbled in his pocket and held out the crumpled bills. “Here, we agreed on five dollars cash money. Take it. You can stay in a fancy hotel for a few days. You'll change your mind after you've had a hot bath and slept in a soft bed."

Clickety Clack stared out over the valley. "You know, Hank, we knights of the road are like family, and family sticks together. You keep that money and do the right thing with it."

Henry realized that Clickety Clack must have figured out how he'd come by the cash.

Clickety Clack was a smart old gentleman.

When he returned the money to his mother, Henry decided he would give her back double the amount he'd taken! That's what a true knight of the road would do.

He nodded in solemn promise. Tears burned the corners of his eyes, spilling over. "I don't want you to go."

"Now, boy, none of that. You knew from the beginning that I rode the rails and I rode 'em alone." Clickety Clack gently laid his hands on Henry's shoulders and looked down into his wet face. “Hank, I want you to know something. You were the first pardner I ever had and you’ve made me see the light. Having a great companion like you is something I could get used to.”

Henry swiped at his cheeks, embarrassed by his babyish tears. “Really?”

“Really. Why, if I hurry, I bet I can hop that freight with Fred Glass and the gang. They’re a good bunch. Now, come on.” He patted Henry on the back. “You go down and find your pa. You’ll have lots of stories to tell about High-handed Hank and old Clickety Clack.”

Henry hiccuped. “When I get home, I’m going to draw a special secret sign on my gatepost just for you.” As he imagined what the symbol might be, Clickety Clack looked at him questioningly. “Don’t worry.” Henry smiled. “You’ll know it when you see it.”

Henry knew Clickety Clack wouldn’t like it, but he gave his friend a big hug, then started down to the valley. When he reached the bottom, he turned to wave, but Clickety Clack was gone. Then he saw a lone figure walking along the rail line on the trestle bridge that crossed the river.

The unmistakable sound of a freight train whistle made Henry turn. A train had rumbled around the hill next to the construction site and was charging straight for the trestle!

Clickety Clack turned to face the oncoming locomotive.

The whistle was now a shriek as the train thundered toward the old man. Henry saw that the hobo couldn't outrun the engine, and there was no escape on the narrow bridge. Clickety Clack was trapped!

Henry watched as his friend climbed onto the edge of the bridge and, with a heart-stopping leap, jumped into nothingness.

The helpless hobo plunged down to the swirling river below.

It was then that Henry remembered Clickety Clack couldn't swim.

This was not how he'd imagined today would go. Everything was supposed to work out for both of them. Henry hadn't come all this way with his friend to watch him drown.

CHAPTER 15

There was only one thing Henry could do. He raced toward the river.

The deep green water looked cold and deadly. Henry's legs shook, but he made himself go on. His eyes swept the part of the river where his friend had landed.

Then he saw him. Clickety Clack was struggling desperately in the middle of the wide stream.

Henry didn't stop to think. He pulled off his shoes and dove headfirst into the murky water. He struck out with a strong sure stroke, using the current to help him reach his drowning friend.

All his swimming skills came back in a

flash. He moved swiftly, but he wasn't fast enough. The old hobo slipped under the frigid water and disappeared. Forcing his muscles to work harder, Henry reached the spot he'd last seen his friend. Taking a deep breath, he dove down, down, down.

Groping in the murky darkness, Henry felt something hit his hand. It was the hobo's old turkey. He clutched at it and pulled. Henry felt the drag of a heavy body. Reaching down, he grabbed Clickety Clack under the arms and yanked him to the surface.

Struggling to keep the old man's face out of the water, Henry pulled him to shore. He dragged the unconscious hobo out of the water, rolled him over and pounded on his back. Clickety Clack's eyes remained closed.

"Come on, you old goat!" Henry pleaded. "This is no time to quit!" He shook the still body, then slapped the hobo's cold cheeks. Henry silently prayed his friend wasn't dead.

Suddenly Clickety Clack coughed, spewing water out of his mouth as he gasped for air.

Henry sat back with a sigh of relief.

“Who you calling an old goat, boy?” Clickety Clack croaked in a raspy voice.

Henry looked down at the soggy tramp and grinned.

Workers who’d seen the rescue swarmed around them, and one man shouted for the doctor. Henry became aware of someone calling his name. He looked up to see his father pushing through the crowd.

His pa ran to him and wrapped him in a bear hug. “Oh my God, Henry, are you all right, son?”

Henry saw fear in his father’s eyes. It was not something he’d ever seen before. “I’m fine,” Henry said, “and so is my friend.” He nodded at Clickety Clack, who was lying on the riverbank, coughing.

A man with a neatly trimmed beard and a worn black bag edged through the crowd and gave Clickety Clack a quick examination. “I’m the project doctor and I think you should come with me to the infirmary. You need to rest, and I’m sure a good night’s sleep and some hot food would do you a world of good.”

Henry knew Clickety Clack wanted to catch the train that Mr. Glass and the other hobos were on. “Oh, I don’t think he’ll need that...”

“Now, let’s not be hasty, boy,” Clickety Clack interrupted. “I’m an old man and that was a long way to fall. I dang near drowned. I think a soft bed and a hot meal are just what the doctor ordered.” He winked at Henry. “There are freight trains leaving Calgary every day.”

They carefully loaded the crafty hobo onto a thick pile of sacks in the back of a wagon. He gave Henry a wide grin. “Well now, Hank, I’ll be ’round your way one of these days, looking for that special sign. We’re family, after all.” As the wagon lumbered away, Clickety Clack stuck a fresh plug of chewing tobacco into his mouth and waved goodbye.

Henry nodded and waved back.

"Henry, what on earth are you doing here?" his father asked as the crowd began to disperse. He looked past his son, searching the riverbank and escarpment. "Where are your mother and sister? How did you find me?"

"Ma and Anne aren't here. That old hobo—his name is Clickety Clack—he traveled with me. We dodged railway bulls and caught a freight out of Winnipeg; got left on a prairie siding after hitting a swarm of 'hoppers; then flat-footed it into Regina, where we jumped on another boxcar and rode the rails to Calgary. Nothing to it." His tone was casual as he explained his extraordinary adventure, but there was pride in his voice as well. The Henry he'd been a couple of weeks ago could never have made such a journey.

But that wasn't all he needed to tell his father. Henry took a deep breath. "The truth is, I made a mistake," he said. "Several actually." He took the five dollars out of his pocket. "This belongs to Mother. I stole it from her the night I ran away and I'm sorry." His father looked at him in surprise. Henry went on to tell him about his mother's illness and how Anne had been sent to stay at the convent and how he was supposed to work on his uncle's fishing boat.

Finally finished, he looked into his father's astonished face. "I didn't want to go to work on the boat, so I came to be with you. I'm a hard worker and I know I'd be useful here. Can I stay?"

His father seemed to mull this over, and then a look of resolve came into his eyes. "No, son, you can't."

Henry swallowed. It wasn't what he'd expected to hear.

"And neither can I. We're both going home. These projects let you work for six weeks, and then they bring in a new crew so some other fellows can earn a wage. You arrived on my last day here." His face became grave. "Henry, I received a letter from your mother and she told me how sick she is. I won't sugarcoat it for you, son. She's got a long uphill battle ahead of her."

Until that moment, Henry hadn't realized how sick his mother really was, and his face must have betrayed his alarm.

"Try not to worry. Your mother's a fighter and I know she'll pull through." A half smile crept across his father's face. "There's good news too. When your mother took Anne to stay with the nuns, they asked if I would be willing to hire on as a permanent handyman at the convent." The rest of the smile showed up. "Your mother said yes, and I'm starting next week. The family will be together again." He paused and the smile faltered. "Well, most of the family, anyway, and it's our job to make sure everything is ticking along when your mother does come home."

Henry was speechless, then he shook his head as a grin curled the edges of his lips. Well, if this wasn't the world's biggest joke on him. His pa would have returned home without Henry coming all the way out here. Now, no matter how long their mother had to stay in the hospital, he and Anne would be able to stay with their father.

"All this comes as quite a shock to me too, but I can see that things have changed." His father laid a hand on Henry's shoulder. "You've changed, son. The Henry Dafoe I left behind would never have done any of the things I've seen and heard today. When you saved that poor man, well, that was a mighty brave thing you did, but when you confessed to taking the money, I knew something was very different. That was something a grown man would do."

Henry saw the pride in his father's eyes and it made everything he'd been through worthwhile.

He wished old Clickety Clack could see him now.

Henry thought of how he'd jumped into the river when his friend had needed his help. Somehow, the idea of all that water didn't bother him anymore. He knew he could handle anything. He felt a lot older and, thanks to Clickety Clack, a lot wiser.

"Let's collect my last paycheck and head home." His father glanced down at him as they made their way to the foreman's building. "It sounds like you've had quite an adventure. You're going to have to tell me the whole story from start to finish."

Henry settled his book bag on his shoulder. "On two conditions..."

His father raised an eyebrow at him. "And what would they be?"

"First," he pulled the letter to Anne out of his book bag, "we mail this to Anne right away so she can get her very first letter, and second..." Henry grinned at his father, "you call me Hank."

Henry's father looked surprised at first. Then he smiled at his son. "You've got yourself a deal, Hank."

As they climbed back up the steep riverbank, Henry thought about his extraordinary adventures and how they rivaled anything in his favorite books. He'd come close to losing his family and his home—not to mention one cantankerous old rod rider—but now he realized how much these things meant to him. He would never turn his back on his family and friends again.

Pirates had their gold, which was mighty tempting, but he had his family and that was worth more than ten chests full of plunder.

Who knew what awaited him? Maybe he'd end up on his uncle's fishing boat after all. Perhaps he'd learn how to steer it and sail the seven seas in a tall ship. Maybe one day he'd follow in Mark Twain's footsteps and work as a riverboat pilot on the mighty Mississippi. Henry knew, after what he'd been through, that anything was possible. A grin spread across his face and he stood a little taller as he matched his father's stride.

This was not how he'd imagined today would go, but sometimes, if you were very lucky, life handed you a surprise, and that was a wonderful thing.

Harris County Public Library
Houston, Texas

Key to the secret signs

A kindhearted woman lives here	A gentleman lives here	Hit the road quick	There are thieves about
Vicious dog	Well-guarded home	A cranky man lives here	An officer of the law lives here
Be quiet!	Road spoiled	Go this way	Housewife will feed you for chores
Generous people	Safe to sleep in the barn	Doctor won't charge for his services	Man with a gun lives here
Fresh water and safe campsite	Work available	Police frown on hobos here	Good place to hang out
Good food but you have to work for it	Dangerous neighborhood	Here you will find friends	Good place to catch a train
A good place for sit-down food	Don't give up	A good road to follow	Henry was here

Jacqueline Guest is the author of more than a dozen books for children, including *Belle of Batoche* (Orca), which was inspired by Jacqueline's family history. When she's not traveling across Canada promoting literacy and the love of books, she's at home in Bragg Creek, Alberta, researching and writing and, of course, reading.